DOCKSIDE
SCHOOL
STORIES

BERNARD ASHLEY

Illustrated by
Elsie Lennox

WALKER BOOKS
AND SUBSIDIARIES
LONDON • BOSTON • SYDNEY

First published 1990 by Julia MacRae Books
as *The Ghost of Dockside School* and *The Caretaker's Cat*

This edition published 1992 by
Walker Books Ltd, 87 Vauxhall Walk
London SE11 5HJ

4 6 8 10 9 7 5

Text © 1990 Bernard Ashley
Illustrations © 1990 Elsie Lennox
Cover illustration © 1992 David Frankland

Printed in England

British Library Cataloguing in Publication Data
A catalogue record for this title is available
from the British Library.
ISBN 0-7445-2305-2

CONTENTS

1 THE GHOST OF DOCKSIDE SCHOOL

There was no way Lee was going to be in the play.
Walking around on the drama blocks with the
stage lights full on and pretending to be someone
else – he'd never be able to hold up his head in
Harding's Court again. But being one of the scene
shifters, that was something else. Done up all in
black like the man in the adverts who sneaks
chocolates up the mountain, who'd take the mick
out of someone like that? And it'd be a laugh, he
reckoned, behind the scenes where you couldn't
be seen.

He got to school very early for the dress
rehearsal; the first in the playground as usual,
waiting with his back to a wall. Dockside School
wasn't the same place at all at night. It had every
light on, all three floors of it, looked like a big
liner on a flat dark sea, going nowhere. But even
with all that light it still looked spooky. The old
turrets shone yellowish in the street lamps, and he

could well imagine murders being done, like in the old Victorian days; he could well imagine the school ghost coming out. It was definitely a different place, and, with no-one to see him do it, he let it make him shiver.

It was more back to normal inside. Inside it was all running round the hall and up the wallbars till Mrs Winterburn got some order and took the actors off to get dressed up. Mr Brewer pulled the stage crew out for a talk: soft voice, don't-let-me-down stuff to get them in the mood. But nothing the man had to say about backstage rules and team spirit made a fraction of the impression on Lee that Linda Evans did when she came walking out of the library dressed up in her old-fashioned clothes. When she'd gone in there with the others he'd been back at school for the laugh. When she came out again his Adam's apple somehow made laughing a hard thing to do.

Lee had grown up with Linda Evans, she'd lived on the next landing in Harding's Court since they were babies. In real life she'd been his friend and his enemy for years; in games she'd been his baby and his dog, someone to shoot at and someone to sit on. She'd been his goal post and he'd been her horse: he knew her so well he never gave her a second look. Until tonight. Tonight when she came out of the library, she really was someone else!

She was the maid in this stupid play. She had to curtsey to her master all the time and she had a funny bit when she had to dust her mistress. Lee hadn't given her a second look in any of the rehearsals except to pass some snide remark to Kenny or whoever was near him. But when he saw her now it was as if his eyes had forgotten how to blink, and going by how dry his mouth was, it must have been hanging open like some thirsty dog's.

She was in a sort of shower cap made of material, and a long dress which made her look sixteen. And Mrs Winterburn had put make-up on her, a line of blue under her eyes and a pale shiny

lipstick. They'd all come out in ones and twos, showing off to everyone else, doing twirls or bows or pretending they weren't any different till someone made them smile: and there were giggles and screeches and a million looks in the mirrors which the hall windows made. But Linda Evans stood quiet, wasn't part of all the fuss, looked as grown-up as she must have felt. And Lee had this funny feeling, a bit like being scared, and suddenly the school wasn't the same place it had ever been before.

Linda shivered at him. "I'nt 'alf cold," she said. "Feel stupid in this old blouse."

"You look stupid." Lee's voice came out high, like an infant's, and he wasn't pleased.

"Botheration!" Mrs Winterburn cut across herself trying to calm the cast. "The Act Two costumes are up in Room Twenty." She seemed to be walking several ways at once. "Stage crew!" She snapped her fingers at Lee. "Run up and check if it's open, will you?" And she was off about another hundred bits of business.

Linda Evans looked at Lee. "Room Twenty!" she mouthed. "You gotta go up there!"

2

Lee stared back, his inside turning at the soft look she seemed to be giving him. Room Twenty! The turret room they didn't use for anything: where old desks and pictures and forgotten bits of work were put after Open Days: and costumes for plays.

The old turret room where the ghost of Dockside School hung out.

There were two turret rooms. They matched, one at each end of the building, on the two top landings before you came to the lofts. Lee tugged at his ear-ring, ran his tongue over his uneven front teeth, the way he did when he tried to look tough, when he wasn't sure about something. The turret room – the one they actually called *The Turret Room* – was no problem at all. That was used for special language work and meetings and had charts and paintings mounted on the walls and all up the inside dome of the ceiling, it didn't have a wasted bit of space. It was bright and lively all day with Mrs Lesley and her special lessons: and no-one minded running up the landings to get there. But the other one was different. The caretaker had put a board across the stairs so you couldn't get to it, he didn't bother cleaning there, and the landing light which had broken had never been replaced. It was the same lay-out, but a very different place: like different landings at Harding's Court. Some you went to, no bother, others you wouldn't go anywhere near.

And Room Twenty wasn't just neglected. It was definitely haunted, everyone in the school knew that; everyone understood why the caretaker wouldn't work there on his own. *Ellie* lived there: or, at least, she *appeared* there, showed herself there to people when they were on their own and tried to make them feel sorry for her. She came – so they said – in the long dress she'd been buried in, the same sort of dress she'd been wearing when she'd reached over the open fire to get to the mantelpiece . . . It was all in the school Log Book; the teachers sometimes read from it when the fourth years did their history of the school. Everyone knew about *Ellie*, the first caretaker's daughter who'd had the run of the building.

"You won't dare go up there."

Linda Evans hadn't been looking at Lee with any softness, she hadn't been feeling sorry at all; what was on her face was more of a twist; or it could have been daring him. It was hard to tell with her looking so different in the make-up.

"Who won't?"

"You won't. You're scared *Ellie*'ll get you!"

"Stupid! Who believes in ghosts?"

"You do."

"Yeah?" And at that moment Lee knew that if ever there was anything he had to do tonight, him in the black like the Black Magic man, it was to show Linda Evans how brave he was: turn that twist in her mouth to a smile. "Ghosts are daft! See me!"

And without thinking about the crazy thing he was doing, Lee went, nearly knocking Mrs Winterburn over as he pushed through the swing doors of the hall to the foot of the turret stairs.

"Steady! No need to fetch anything, just try the door," Mrs Winterburn called. "No need to go in."

"Don't worry, miss! He won't!" he heard Linda Evans shout.

3

The hall doors swung-to like someone dusting
their hands of him, and Lee, part-way up to the
first half-landing, suddenly thought about what he
was doing. Already, just this little way away, the
sounds of the rehearsal had faded, as if that were
of one world, and outside here was of another.
The lights on the lower stairs were dim, and there
were no beckoning noises from the hall and
classrooms above, nothing to make him feel like it
was normal and daytime. He'd run up there
without thinking in the day. But it was night, and
he was on his own going up to the turret, and up
there *Ellie* the ghost could come out and get him.

Get him? Lee kept his feet going up slowly
while his thoughts raced ahead. *Get* him? Get *him*?
He tried to cheer himself up. What could she do
even if there was an *Ellie*? He could beat up
anyone in the school except Big Eddie if he
wanted to, and he could definitely sort out the

girls. So why should he be scared of what some old-fashioned dead ghost could do? Huh! But his steps were getting slower and slower. Did you feel it if a ghost walked right through you? Was it like an x-ray, or did it hurt as it went? Would it be cold, or clammy; or would the very look of her scare him out of his head anyway? Did ghosts look normal, like they had before they died; or did they look like something terrible had happened to them? Who was that queen who walked round with her head tucked underneath her arm? Could she put it back on her neck when she wanted to? Would *Ellie* look scary or not?

Lee was on the third landing now, with three more to go. He'd passed the upper hall, and he was going into hard heart-beat territory. Even in the daylight kids didn't like coming up here, not unless they'd got all their mates with them: no-one did.

And here he was! He thought of Linda Evans, with that *Lee's a chicken* look on her face: on her different, grown-up face. And suddenly finding it hard to breathe, a weird feeling like having his uncle's strong arms pinning him round the chest,

he crept round the last corner before the dreaded Room Twenty.

The little screen which was normally kept across the stairs was pushed to one side; and there above him was the old, cream-painted door. He had slowed to the sort of pace at which people climb a rock face, the position of each hand and each foot most carefully considered. The door knob was on his eye-level now, old and brass and dented as if hands had gripped it at some time in the past and crushed the shape out of it.

He reached out, gripped the knob himself, felt the dents in his palms. And he stopped. He was there. He'd got this far at least. For most kids what he'd done up to now had been enough, he thought; he'd come to the top of the turret and he'd put his hand on *Ellie*'s door handle. What more would anyone do, even for a dare?

4

Well, he knew what more. He had to see if the room was open, to see whether or not Mrs Winterburn would have to send for Mr Toombs the caretaker to come out of the pub over the road and unlock it for her. There was nothing else for it. Linda Evans' smile mocked him. He had to turn that handle. If he didn't he couldn't give her any answer – and no-one would believe he'd even got this far. Linda Evans would think he'd bottled it; and he wasn't having her think that.

So. Lee got a grip on the knob and forced himself to think about something really ordinary and normal. He thought about his big Uncle Rod lying with one leg over the side of the armchair, swearing at some idiot on the telly. He thought how the man would laugh if he could see him right now, too scared to turn a door knob and see if a stupid room was locked. What wouldn't he call him if he knew?

Lee turned the knob. It was locked. Good! His hand flew off it as if it were charged with electricity. He could go back now: no-one could make him wrong.

Or could they? He'd turned it to the right, hadn't he, and it hadn't moved. What if the knob went to the left? He had to try to the left. He was in a sweat now, and cross because he knew he wasn't done after all. He'd look a right idiot if they sent for old Toombs and the door turned out to be unlocked. They'd think he'd lied – bottled it enough to lie.

Lee turned the knob to the left.

No! Mum! It turned. It went that way. What dead rotten luck! Now he had to push the door to see whether or not it was locked. And a sudden thought caught him like a blow, had his arm trembling as he held on. Even if he only made a little crack . . . the ghost could slip through that, couldn't she?

Stupid! She could slip through anything if she was a ghost, door and walls and anything! What was he on about? Angry with himself now for being in such a state, Lee pushed the door, not hard, just in case: but he pushed it – and it gave.

And the shock was, the light was on, as if someone was up there already. Lee went very, very cold, felt the sweat at his hair roots turn to ice. But, nothing. No-one. As he looked around the room from the doorway his heart-beat slowed, and he began to feel on top. When the caretaker had got the other costumes down he must have forgotten the light. And you didn't get ghosts in

the light, not the electric, they were much more old-fashioned than that. Gas, yes; candles: but not under a neon strip. No chance. The thought made him bold. He'd show Linda Evans – properly. He'd find a way to make her look at him like he was sixteen too.

He pushed the door and went right in; not just in, but right in with a big step. He looked round with his hands on his hips as if he owned the place. No problem.

And his guts jumped out through his eyeballs as a loud crack whacked-off behind him. Help! He spun round, fists raised ready to face the ghost, to punch her, kick at her, push through her and run.

But there was nothing there; no-one, neither dead nor alive, just the door where it had swung back and hit the wall when he'd pushed it. Lee's heart choked his breathing whilst his stomach twisted in him like a fairground pain. Stupid again! He wouldn't tell anyone about that.

But what could he tell Linda to prove he'd been right into the room? Otherwise it was all wasted, being brave.

Lee looked around. The rack of costumes for the

Second Act were hanging there in front of him, ready to be brought out. Behind them were the old desks he expected to see, and a couple of old-fashioned tin machines a bit like magic lanterns, and chairs, and rolls of old material, and dusty boxes with broken models from the infants, and a P.E. basket of punctured plastic balls that were never going to get repaired. Nothing much. Nothing ghostly, no old gas brackets or fireplaces or corner cupboards in the walls to tell her about. In fact, it was really stupid how people got scared about this room, he thought. It was just an old store for stuff no-one had taken the trouble to throw away, just like the lock-up to his mum's flat.

And there was an old typewriter, a really old one, tall and heavy-looking, with brass rings round the keys, and letters you could hardly read. Metal levers coming up long and curvy like the legs of spiders lying on their backs, and a ribbon looking like a thin black bandage.

Why not? That was it! That'd do, he thought. He looked round for a piece of paper. He'd prove to Linda Evans he'd been up here. He'd do her a message, leave it in the typewriter, then get her to come with the rest when they carried the costumes up.

But he'd better be quick. He had a job to do backstage when all this malarky was over. He'd change that look on Linda's face, though; he'd make her smile at him properly before she wiped that lipstick off tonight.

There was a piece of white paper on the floor, with a dusty footprint on it. So what: as long as she could read his message through it? He put the paper into the roller, twisted it round, got it more or less straight; and then he had a think. What to say? What to say?

To L.E: I was here, on my own. Well, that was the bones of it. And then before he signed it he added, with a flutter just a bit stronger than a ghost might have brought on, *Wish you'd been up here with me*. He pushed the typewriter further back into a corner, where only someone sent to look at it would see the secret message, and leaving the light on he ran out of the room, slammed the door, and got down three flights before he turned round and yelled back up the stairs, "Ghosts are daft!" Yeah! he thought. They really were . . .

5

Downstairs, things didn't seem to be going too badly. Being a dress rehearsal, everyone who was in it was either on the stage or watching, stiff and strange in the hall in their make-up and costumes. The people working the hardest as Lee ran back into the hall were Mr Brewer and the stage crew who were getting to grips with the change at the end of the first scene, turning a fireplace round to become a kitchen stove. Mr Winterburn was up a ladder fixing the lights and giving suggestions to his wife which all began with "Far be it for me to . . . " and Mrs Winterburn was cocking a deaf ear to most of that: while the cast were spending a lot of time with their hands on their hips, waiting.

Linda Evans still looked very special. Lee wondered if she'd ever be the same as she had before, the kid he'd as soon hit as look at. He went over to her, just stopped himself from turning her round by the shoulder, used words instead to coax her.

"Oi! Linda!"

She turned.

"Been up there, in that room."

"Oh, yeah?" She didn't believe him: Harding's Court liar! said her eyes.

"Just gonna tell Winterburn."

"I'nt you brave?"

"Went in there, right in."

"You and whose army?"

"What you mean? On my own! Nothing to it. Nothing in there, only them clothes and a few old bits and pieces."

"Yeah? You knew that anyhow – don't prove you went in." Her weight was on one foot now, like her trust in what he was saying.

"I did an' all. You have a look. There's some old typewriter in there. Writ you a message on it."

"Get off!" She didn't believe a word of it.

"Wanna come up and see, then? If you ain't too scared?"

"Not going up on my own with you. Worse'n the ghost, you'd be!" But perhaps the look on her face wasn't totally out of favour. Before any decision could be made, though, Mrs Winterburn had made up her mind what was to happen next. When Lee told her the door was open, she marshalled her cast, called her husband down from up his ladder, and led everyone who needed an Act Two costume up the stairs after her. So Linda Evans went – but Lee wasn't allowed. Mr Brewer called him, gave him his orders for helping with the scenery.

"Typewriter!" Lee just had time to hiss.

It wasn't long before all the cast came trooping back, everyone talking about *Ellie*, of course, but nothing really scary, not with Mr and Mrs Winterburn around. Lee's eyes were all for Linda: and he got her to one side the second she came back through the door.

"Well?" he said. "See it, did you? See my message?"

"Yeah, I did, as it happens." She hitched her new costume on her arm.

Lee looked at her hard. So, what had she made of it? Hadn't he been brave in going in and typing it? And what about the cheeky message itself, telling her he'd have liked to be up there with her on her own . . ?

"I'nt you a big 'ead?"

"Who?"

"You!" She dropped her voice. "What you wrote."

Lee's mouth went dry, and his throat felt as if he'd got a stone in it. "Nothing wrong if I like you . . ." Was that him? He'd never said anything like that in his life before: never wanted to, never thought to, and here it was coming out as if he were one of those men in the films. He knew how red he must have gone, but even as he stared at her somehow he didn't mind. He'd said it now, hadn't he? She could call him a name and walk off if she liked, but he'd said it: what he wanted to say. "Only said it would've been all right if you'd been up there an' all."

"Yeah? And the rest. Putting them words in my mouth."

"What words? I only said what I said . . ."

Linda Evans stared at him. "And what about that muck you reckoned I'd write back? Big man?"

"What muck? I dunno. I never writ nothing supposed to be down to you."

"No? Then you wanna look, son. Go up and have a look. Then come back and tell me you ain't big-headed!" And Linda had gone, swept off with the others to change for the Second Act, with just half a look back as she pushed through the library door.

6

The bad news for Lee was Mrs Winterburn. There was no earthly reason, she told Lee in the short-tempered voice she was using on her husband by now, why he should have to go upstairs again. He'd do better to concentrate on learning the scene changes properly: opening night was only tomorrow, wasn't it? So that was that.

Unfortunately, there was no getting to Room Twenty in school time, either. The screen was back across the stairs when Lee had a look the next day, and Mr Toombs was always at the bank, it seemed. Even Mrs Winterburn got cross with the man when she wanted to check whether one of the belts had fallen off up there. So it would have to wait until that evening. Lee would just have to be patient to see what Linda Evans was making up about his message on the machine.

He mooned round her all day, not too close, but never too far away, just in case she wanted to join

him in a game or a chat. And she *was* different.
She wore the same school clothes she usually did,
and she wasn't in her make-up; but she was older
all the same, and prettier; she wasn't any different,
but she was very different; it was all in Lee's eyes
and mind. And she was still very nose-in-the-air.
What could she reckon he'd said on that
typewriter?

As soon as they were let into the building the
following night, Lee was up to Mrs Winterburn
and volunteering to go to Room Twenty to look
for the missing belt.

"On your own?" Mrs Winterburn asked him,
disbelievingly. She knew that room's reputation,
everyone did. "Going right in?"

"Yeah! I don't mind!"

"Very well, then. I do want that belt. But – "
Her face looked as if she might be going to say
something about the ghost, but she obviously
changed her mind. "Here's the key." Mr Toombs
had finally trusted her with it. "Don't be long.
Take care."

"Yes, miss." Lee took the key. He didn't quite
like the sound of that. *Take care*! But then he'd

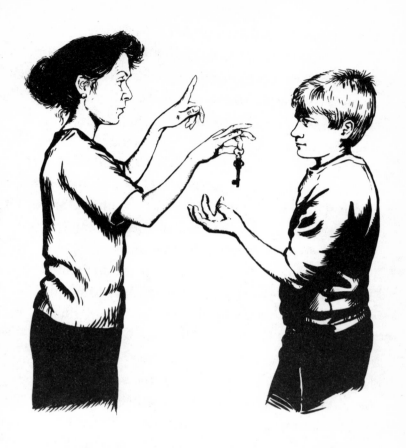

been in there, hadn't he, proved there was nothing
to be scared about. It was all talk, this ghost
business, he knew that better than anyone. Room
Twenty wouldn't be any different to the night

before, and he could prove to Linda Evans that he wasn't the big-head she reckoned he was – just someone with a bit of guts, thank you very much.

All the same, he didn't like the feel of the key. It was old, it had turned that lock for a hundred years or so, he reckoned. And *Ellie*, the old caretaker's daughter, she would have held it in her hand, wouldn't she? The real-life *Ellie*, no messing about with ghosts . . . That made him think: and suddenly the key felt hot, and the next second it felt cold as Lee's hands clammed and chilled and clammed again. His mind changed like his hands and he went from being brave as a lion to wishing he'd never got into all this. He'd shouted 'Ghosts are daft!' coming down, hadn't he? What if there *was* one and she bore a grudge the way Linda Evans could, saved up a kick in the knee or a skeleton hand groping at the heart, sort of thing.

And the same as the night before, after starting off running at them boldly, Lee found himself going up the stairs like an up passenger on a down escalator. Why had he got himself into all this, just because he'd gone soft on stupid Linda Evans?

7

Of course, the last bit going up to the turret was
the worst. The board was across the stairs again,
and the top set of lights was off. When he tried to
find them Lee discovered that all these stairs and
landing lights were worked by a little key with two
prongs which went into light-switch slits; only for
use by the caretaker. And since not a lot of light
came round corners, coming up to the door with
the battered brass knob was done in a spooky
gloom which deepened and darkened the closer
he got.

He found the keyhole. And the sound of the key
going in turned him over; made him feel like a
jailer in a dungeon. He shivered. Anyway – who
cared, he suddenly thought, if Linda Evans *did*
think he was a big-headed coward? Wouldn't be
the end of the world, would it?

But he pushed himself on. One second he was
fighting his cowardice with brave thoughts and

common sense – like hearing Uncle Rod laughing at him – and the next he was all but giving in to the ghost and ready to jump those stairs behind him a million at a time.

Going on won, though, and he turned the key with a final rattle and pushed open the door like someone at a cemetery gate.

The light inside wasn't on tonight. The room was dark, with just the yellow glow of the street lamps filtering through the grime on the windows. Pigeons cooed somewhere near; and if it wasn't their feet scratching then it was rats . . .

Squinting his eyes – and hoping to heaven he wouldn't grope his hand onto some cold face, he felt for the light switch: and thankfully found it, no problem. But when he put it on, the neon took a lifetime of flashing and buzzing, his heart flashing and buzzing along with it: and the light wouldn't work, not properly. Tonight it wasn't as bright as it had been before: it was low and gloomy like an old gas lamp: like it must have been when . . .

Lee shivered and buried the thought deep.

Typewriter. Right! Where was it? All he had to

do was pull the paper out of it and run it downstairs. Then when he was safe he could argue the toss with Linda Evans over what he was supposed to have typed.

The typewriter was where he'd left it. The paper was still in it. Lee didn't hang about. He scrambled it out of the machine and ran with it fluttering like a cheap white flag back past the board and down the stairs at a hundred miles an hour. If there was a record for the Turret Stairs Downhill Event, Lee took it that night, and his record would stand for a hundred years. He left the light on, the key in, and the door wide open – and he went like Tam O'Shanter back to the hall to wave the paper under Linda Evans' nose.

8

But he didn't get past the hall door. Miss Lewin was there, counting her programmes. "Not this door, Lee Brackett. Round the back, helpers."

He'd almost forgotten. There was a play going off in there; and the early ones were sitting on the front titchy chairs already. He ran on down the corridor through the nursery area and came round backstage. Everywhere there was shushing and shivers. "Be quiet!" was being said so often it could have been the name of the play. And of course he couldn't get into the girls' dressing room to show the paper to Linda, so when Mr Brewer loomed he had to shove it in his pocket.

Lee went with him, felt important as the two of them set the stage for Act One. The teacher talked to him as if he were another grown-up, wanted his opinion for real on whether they should twist the fireplace round a bit, or was it all right as it was? Lee said twist it, so they did, no questions to Mrs

Winterburn once Lee had decided, and he was delighted to have been asked. He pulled himself tall, felt a part of this production; and definitely wasn't worried about Room Twenty any more. This was real, and he had really been useful.

There was nothing to do for a bit, and a good twenty minutes to go before the start. So Lee found a corner where he would see Linda Evans coming out of the dressing room, and he pulled the typewritten paper from his pocket. He read it, went over how he'd show it to the girl.

To L.E: I was here, on my own. Wish you'd been up here with me. Signed L.B. That was all right. That was what he'd put.

To L.B: If only I really was. Truly, L.E.

Strewth! Lee pulled it closer to his eyes, read it again, read the print off the paper almost. What was this? This wasn't what he'd written! Well, the first part was, but not the other bit. That had been put on after, where part of the dusty footprint was.

In a cartoon film, Lee's heart would have come pounding out of his black top, *thump, thump, thump, thump,* this side and that: thumping with surprise, with shock, then thumping with pleasure at what Linda Evans had done. She had gone up there with Mrs Winterburn to get the costumes, she'd put her bit on the message, and then made some excuse to get Lee to go and find out what she'd said. The way he had tried to tell her something nice, she had done the same. Two love notes! He went all weak, legs like school soup.

Come on! Lee urgently wanted her out of that dressing room so that he could laugh at her trick and thank her for what she'd typed. And he could wish her good luck for her acting. And wishing an actress good luck, it wasn't out of order to kiss her on the cheek, was it? His chest went tight at the thought. Somehow it seemed like she'd let him.

"Belt? Lee, where's the belt?" It was Mrs Winterburn, changed into her own evening dress for sitting at the piano, fingers going in little notes in the air – and nervous. "The belt, boy! You went to get it, and we need it!"

Linda Evans came out of the dressing room and passed behind Mrs Winterburn, but Lee daren't shift gleam or glint to show her he knew she was there, while Mrs Winterburn went on at him in a voice too loud for backstage. "Go and get it, lad!

We need it. Forget stupid ghosts and *get it*!"

Oh, no! Idiot! That was what he was supposed to have gone up there for. His excuse for going had gone right out of his head as he'd come rushing back down.

Pushing hard, he ran through the nursery, past people paying to come in, got a look to kill from Miss Lewin, and raced for the turret stairs again.

Right, then! One last time. Straight up and straight back: and thank God he'd left the door wide open and the light on, because this really was going to be done in a flash. It was the last thing in the world he wanted to do, but if he could still get back to wish Linda luck, then he wouldn't mind. Yeah! he thought. Think of that good excuse for a kiss! With that waiting for him he'd run in and out on any stupid old ghost . . .

9

And the room was just the same as he'd left it, the light left on, and the door wide open. He ran up and ran in trying not to think, but so ready to go back down that his muscles were all set for the turn and the run the opposite way.

Except he had to find that blessed belt. But luck, it seemed, was with him. There it was in such full view on the floor that he wondered how he'd forgotten it before. One quick scoop and he was turning to go.

"*Hello, boy*," a girl's voice suddenly said. "*You forgot something! I thought you might come back.*"

Lee's legs drained out through the cracks in the floorboards. It was like bad dreams he'd had – when Uncle Rod or his mum had had to come in and tell him to grow up. His blood had turned to something in the freezer, his brain to stone. But he had to look. He wanted to run like hell, but he had to look.

And when he did he could have killed Linda Evans. Never mind having a fancy on her, he'd have liked to give her his boot – because there she was, standing in the corner in her old-fashioned costume, keeping her face in a shadow to try to scare him by looking like *Ellie*, the ghost. But he knew who it was, she couldn't change her voice, even with her hand up in front of her face.

What did she think he was, stupid? He'd seen her go, sliding past Mrs Winterburn when she'd sent him back up here for the belt. She'd heard it all and come on up here to scare him.

"Clever, i'nt you?" he told her. "Coming up here to put the frights up me! And all I ever said to you was nice, blinkin' nice . . ."

"Don't take on, boy. Don't shout at Ellie. Left you a message to read, didn't I?" She had turned back again, was holding out her arms the way everyone reckons ghosts do, was going to come towards him. All she needed was a stupid sheet over her head.

"Get lost, Evans!" Lee yelled back, aiming a kick which somehow went nowhere. "I'll show you! I'll show you who's gonna look the stupid fool! Wait till Winterburn's looking for you!" And in a quick, sudden move he dashed for the door, slammed it behind him with a crash to shake the turret off, turned the key in the lock and ran off down the stairs. Now see her made-up, grown-up face when he let her out! After they'd had to hold up the start till she was found! Now see the trouble she'd get from Winterburn for trying to make him look like a scared little kid.

10

Past a tut-tutting Lewin and backstage once again, Lee found Mrs Winterburn. He managed to give her the belt as if that were the only thing he'd ever had on his mind.

"Thank you!" she said tartly. "You cut it fine. Got no idea of time, some of you! Overture and beginners!" she called over her shoulder to Mr Brewer – and she swept through the curtain to polite applause and the rather hurried dimming of the hall lights by her husband which had her barking her shin against the piano stool.

Lee looked at the clock. No! It was starting time already, past it. He'd been upstairs tons longer than he thought. And he hadn't just dropped Linda Evans into trouble ready to pull her out again – he'd left her where there was no chance of her being found before it all went wrong. Not without going out there and stopping Mrs Winterburn bashing away at the piano.

The once brave Lee, the twice and thrice brave Lee now decided to bottle it. He couldn't go out there and do that! They'd have to find out Linda wasn't there when she didn't turn up on the stage – and he'd have to take what was coming when the all-off happened. There was just no way he was creeping out in front of all those people and gently letting down the piano lid on Winterburn's flying fingers.

With a rush of cool air and audience noise and dust the curtains opened and the play began. The master and the mistress of the Victorian household started to say their lines. It had all got out of hand. Moaning about the soot in the fireplace, Wendy Kent was going on about getting rid of the servant girl, sending her back to the country. She rang the bell by the mantelpiece for Linda to come.

Gritting his teeth, screwing up his face, making himself as small and as invisible as he could, Lee waited for the pause, the wait and the awkwardness when the girl didn't come to answer it. He waited for Mrs Winterburn to have to jump up and find out what was going on, because Linda Evans as the maid would not be walking in. He measured the distance between where he was crouching and the nursery, and the school door and the outside world. He thought how, if he went now, he could be home indoors with *Dallas* by the time the explosion went off: he could just about be in bed and pretending to be asleep by the time they heard Linda Evans screaming to be let out of the Turret Room.

He felt in his pocket. He still had the key. Should he drop it on the floor or take it with him? He didn't know. He dropped it down behind a radiator; then fished it out again, left it on a chair where it could be seen. They'd need it, because he'd definitely locked her in . . .

His inside turned and his cheeks went tight. He'd really done it now!

He was so nervous he didn't hear her voice, not at first. But what was that? Up on the stage? What was Linda Evans saying? *Linda Evans*? He looked up, couldn't believe his ears, had to try his eyes. And there she was, as large as life, going through her lines, doing her funny part where she dusted the mistress, and getting a laugh with it, smiling at the audience all pleased and happy.

Lee fell back. He fell over against the radiator, hurt himself but didn't have the breath in him to swear.

"Sssh!" said Mr Brewer.

But Lee didn't shush. "Strewth!" he said in a disbelieving voice which could be heard at the back of the school hall. And after he'd been marched in whispers to one of the classrooms by Mr Brewer, treating him like a kid again, all he could do was sit there and mouth over and over, "I've seen a ghost! I've seen a ghost! I've seen that *Ellie*!" Either that, or there was more than one

key, or the lock didn't work, or there was another
way out of that room.

But he dare not ask Linda Evans. Somehow he
didn't want to know for sure. And thank goodness

she'd be out of that costume and make-up at school tomorrow: she'd be back to normal again. But he never ever wanted to look over her work, never ever wanted to see her initials on anything. L.E: which could either stand for *Linda Evans*, or be the way some old ghost thought her name was spelt, done quick on a new invention like a typewriter.

THE CARETAKER'S CAT

1

Miranda Finch watched them through the strands
of her hair – the way she watched things at
home – her head bent over what she was
supposed to be doing, but her eyes on who was
talking. The two men were carrying on as if she
weren't there, or as if she were deaf, or as if she
spoke some different language.

"Look at it! On my suit!" Mr Holt was saying,
looking not at all like a headteacher as he stuck
out his bottom to pull cat's fur off the shine of
his trousers.

The caretaker was already looking down at the
area of complaint.

"You've sat where a cat's been," he said,
picking off a bit of fluff himself, forcing Mr Holt
to stand up straight, on his dignity.

"Mr Toombs, I know I've sat where a cat's
been! That's the point! But where have I sat
where a cat's been? That's the question!"

Mr Toombs shook his head as if he were in a quiz being asked something too hard to answer.

"I'll tell you. In here. On my chair. Over there." The headteacher pointed to his place on the opposite side of the desk to where Miranda was sitting. "It's got to be your cats, Mr Toombs – after school, when you've given them the run of the place."

Mr Toombs shook his head. "Oh no, I'm very strict with my cats. They know better than to come in here, Mr Holt. They never do what they're not supposed to ..."

"Then they're a sight brighter than the children. I tell you, Mr Toombs, I can smell them in the mornings." He sniffed the air, as if to show the caretaker what smelling meant.

Mr Toombs shook his head again. "More than their life's worth, to come in here. Must be a stray, got in the window."

"On the fourth landing? Half-way up the turret?"

"Very determined, cats."

"Well, so am I. I'm very determined they're not coming in here again. It's not their school, it's

mine. You tell your cats and their friends to stay in the playground, please."

"Well, I'll do my best."

"Thank you." Mr Holt wriggled his shoulders in his jacket, flexed his neck, sort of shook himself back to the job in hand. "All right, then." He stared across at Miranda, reached in his jacket for his pencil.

"Hang on." Mr Toombs dropped his voice. "Bend over again."

Without thinking, Mr Holt did, while Mr Toombs picked off a bit more fur, dusted him down. "There you go."

"Thank you very much."

At which Miranda nearly fell off her chair.

"And what are you finding so funny, young lady?"

Miranda sat up tall, her face dead straight again. "Thought he was gonna kick you one," she said. Quite matter of fact, because that's what she would have done.

"Well then, it's a good job we're not all like you, isn't it? Have you finished that sum?"

Miranda sighed. "Too 'ard," she said.

Mr Holt sighed, too. "No, it's not. You don't give yourself a chance. Thank you, Mr Toombs. Now, let's have a look …"

2

Miranda didn't know why she did some things.
They seemed a good idea at the time, and she
just didn't seem to have that brake inside which
most people have to hold them back. If she
thought someone's hair would be good for pulling,
she pulled it. If her nails felt scratchy and she
saw a bare arm or a smooth face, she'd scratch.
And if someone was black-skinned, tall, thin,
fat or bald she'd call it after them: teacher
or dinner lady or kid as big as they liked.

Well, at school, anyhow. Things like that didn't
happen at home. If they happened at home she
just got hit, and their hitting really hurt: so at
home she sat quiet in corners, and her dad and
her mum didn't know what they were on about
up at the school about her being naughty. They
ran their car scrap business under the railway
arches and they didn't really *want* to know. And
with a mum as big as her dad, Miranda never

stepped out of line: she never stepped anywhere. So her behaviour was only a problem at the school: and it was only the school trying to solve it.

Mr Holt thought her problem was due to her not being very good at reading and maths. If she could do those things better, he told people, she wouldn't need to prove herself all the time through being bad. The trouble was, with big classes and not enough teachers, it was hard to find ways to bring her on. She had special needs – but her parents wouldn't give permission for anyone from outside to help her. So, short of excluding her from school, there wasn't much Mr Holt could do except try to help her himself. When he could. When time and what he called his 'mountain of paper' permitted.

The first time Miranda had gone to him she'd looked for it in his room – his mountain of paper. She knew it wouldn't be the size of a real mountain – she wasn't daft – but she did think she'd see a model-sized one. Something covered in coloured tissue: or made of painted papier-mâché. But there wasn't anything in his room except

letters and folders and files and books, and she
started to wonder if he hadn't been telling pork
pies. But she said nothing, didn't stir anything, in
case he stopped her coming, because she liked it
in his room. For every two minutes work there
were ten minutes waiting while Mr Holt
telephoned someone or saw Mrs Spencer-Craft, the
secretary, and she heard about all sorts of things
the rest of the school didn't. Like this trouble

with the caretaker's cats, and why Mrs
Winterburn was sometimes late. And it was good
having someone who smiled at her, even if she
did think he was a wally and in her head she was
thinking all the time what the kids sang about
him:

"Holt, Holt, hundred volt,
blow your fuse,
an' all your fault."

3

Right now, though, there were no distractions.
The cat and the caretaker business seemed over
and they were going through a quiet ten minutes.
Through the just-open door, she could hear the
electric typewriter bleeping in the office. In here,
Mr Holt was round on Miranda's side of the table
working with her. In front of them was a sheet of
squared paper with coloured locking cubes laid on
it. And under the cubes was the sum she couldn't
do, written down.

"Look – when we've got ten of these units" –
Mr Holt pressed them together to make a little
multi-coloured rod – "what have we got?" He
waved the rod in front of her.

"A magic wand?"

"No! Don't be silly! We've got a ..."

Miranda stared at him, twitched her nose.

"We've got a ... *ten*, haven't we? A *ten*. What
have we got?"

"A *ten*."

"Good." He laid it down. "And when I put our ten into the next column, what have I got left?" He stood up, lent over to flick the remaining units closer. "What have I got left behind?"

Miranda wanted to say cat's fur, on your trousers, but she knew that would have got her sent straight back to her classroom. So she counted the units. "Eight," she said.

"No ..."

"Nine."

"No. Don't guess. Count."

"Seven."

"Correct! See, and we write it down like this."

Mr Holt pulled out what he called his helping pencil; and while he wrote down the seven for what seemed his own benefit, at that moment Miranda's younger, sharper ears picked up something he didn't hear. The slight squeak of an opening door.

She looked round.

"No, here!" He tapped the pencil on the paper.

Miranda looked back at the paper, but then she was round at the door again, because she had seen what she had seen: and he wouldn't pick on her for looking at what had just come in.

" 'Old it. 'Ere, look!" she dragged his pencil hand away.

Mr Holt looked himself: he, too, came back to the paper, then shot round at the door again. His mouth dropped open as they both watched what came walking in, a sleek-backed black cat with the biggest belly going. And they both knew without checking, going by the fur they'd seen before, that this was the culprit cat who'd been sitting on his chair.

"Charlie!" Miranda said. "Toombs's cat."

"*Mr* Toombs's cat." Mr Holt was still staring. "It can't be called *Charlie*! It's female. That's nine months pregnant, that cat."

"Nine *weeks*. Nine *weeks*, cats carry."

"You know what I mean."

They both stared to see what she would do: but only because she was pregnant, Miranda reckoned. The mood Holt Volt had been in, she would have gone out of the door with a toe up her tail if she hadn't been about to be a mother.

The sum forgotten, they watched: while calmly, unhurried, as if everything had been planned in advance, the pregnant cat walked along the kerb of the fireplace and came to the door of the alcove cupboard. It was an old-fashioned cupboard divided into two, with a top half and a bottom half, painted cream and dotted with drawing-pin holes like woodworm. And with a skilful paw she hooked round the lower door and pulled it open.

Mr Holt straightened up, swallowed, and went on watching.

Inside the cupboard a line of old box files stood on end, leaving a space at one side. But as if

she'd only been checking on it, the cat turned and back-tracked across to Mr Holt's easy chair on the other side of the fireplace. Suddenly she jumped up and worried at the newspaper lying there.

Now Mr Holt decided to move. Enough was enough, pregnant cat or not. "Leave that! That's today's!" he commanded.

"Don't matter. Hold on!" Miranda grabbed his arm. "Just you watch."

And for some weird reason, the headteacher shut his mouth and obeyed her.

4

Together they watched the cat claw and tear an
outer page off his *Guardian* and drag it in her
teeth over to the cupboard she had opened. They
watched her scratching and shredding and walking
round and round upon herself while she padded
the paper down on the cupboard bottom. And
they went on watching while the cat went back to
fetch more pages, then more again, leaving a tatty
trail across the room in a line of litter, each time
walking round and round inside the cupboard and
settling it down.

Finally, they saw Charlie the pregnant cat stay
where she was inside the cupboard and curl
herself up on her newspaper bed.

"What the devil's going on?" Mr Holt asked.
"You've had me standing here watching that cat
take over my blessed cupboard!"

"That's why you got fur on your trousers,"
Miranda told him. "Why she was in here – on

your chair."

"What do you mean?" All at once the world
was upside down, Miranda was teaching the
headteacher.

"She came in last night and picked it, didn't
she? Picked a dark place for her nest."

"Nest? She's a cat, Miranda, not a bird! Even
Mr Toombs's cat knows what she's supposed
to be."

"It's what they call it, a nest. It's for having
her babies. They all do it – pick a dark place to
have 'em, then they make it all comfy."

"Oh." Mr Holt accepted that: until what that meant suddenly dawned upon him. "But she can't take over my cupboard for having her kittens! I can't have her *producing* in here. I have visitors in this room. I have to work." He pointed at the box files. "I've got to be able to get at the National Curriculum!" He grabbed at the telephone and pushed a button with such force it looked as if he were blowing something up. "Would you bleep Mr Toombs, please? Tell him I want him up here *immediately*."

Miranda sat back and watched, dangled her arm over the back of her chair. Mr Holt bent and peered at the cat, straightened up, and then bent and peered again. In between, he shot impatient looks at the office door, at his watch. Miranda watched him. It looked as if the man was saying things inside his head which she mustn't be allowed to hear. Any second now and he'd have to send her out, for the secretary to take back to her class.

But she was lucky. She had been forgotten, too. Mr Holt was beginning to bang things about on his desk. He kept saying, "Ye Gods!" He yanked

up the phone again. "Is he coming?" he snarled, and slammed it down and walked to the door and back. Miranda knew things wouldn't have got this far back at home, under the arches. The cat would have gone out of the door sideways, the air would have been thicker with words than with diesel fuel, and old Toombs would have shown his face miles quicker − and still gone home with it changed if he'd tried to argue the toss.

Miranda leaned sideways in her chair, shifted her arm along the table. From there she saw Charlie lying licking her fur and breathing very big: not looking a bit like the cats they had at home. She was a pet, while those at the yard were only there to keep the rats down: tough cats which you didn't stroke and which hardly needed feeding.

There was a knock at the door. She shot up straight, and so did Mr Holt.

"Come!"

And Miranda quickly hunched down low again. Now for the explosion!

5

Mr Toombs came in. He must have been warned about the mood in here because he didn't try to smile, didn't come in with some smart remark. He just came. The first thing he seemed to see, though, wasn't Mr Holt stretching his mouth all ways but the trail of tattered newspaper from the easy chair across the fireplace to the cupboard.

"Oh, no!" The caretaker said, polite, but firm. He pointed at Miranda. "She done it, she can pick it up. I'm not here for her!"

Miranda spun a look at Mr Holt, then at the wall, at the window, and back at Mr Toombs. That wasn't her, no way she'd done that! She started to say so, found the right words no problem.

"Be quiet, Miranda!" Mr Holt was pointing at the cat cupboard, angrier still now, his hand starting to shake. "Look! Look in there!"

Mr Toombs went forward, bent over gingerly,

got ready to look in the cupboard as if what he was going to see inside could be something so horrible it could give him a heart attack. He seemed very relieved when it was only his cat.

"Well, would you believe it? Would you Adam-'n-Eve it? The little monkey ..." The look on his face was like someone thinking an aspirin was a Tic Tac and chewing on it.

"It's not a little monkey, Mr Toombs, it's a fat cat. It's a pregnant cat and it's made its nest in there ..."

"Nest? Funny old word." The caretaker tried to laugh. "She's not a bird, she's a −"

Miranda thought Mr Holt was going to start jumping up and down. "You told me your cats never come in here −"

"Well, they don't ..."

"*Then what is that?*"

"Not normally, they don't. But females − they go funny when they're going to ..." Mr Toombs looked at Miranda, as if she shouldn't hear about giving birth. "You *know* ..."

"*I'll* go funny in a minute, Mr Toombs!" The skin on Mr Holt's head was showing red through his hair. "Now, will you please get that cat out of here, and then come back and put me straight?" Miranda knew he meant his room, of course, but looking at him it did seem as if his anger had turned him back-to-front inside his suit.

"Yes, sir. Course. Sorry about all this." He smiled warmly, even at Miranda, and he bent to pick the cat out of the cupboard. "Come on, girl.

Come on, you little monkey . . ."

But Charlie didn't want to go. She scratched and she bit and she tried to hang onto her newspaper nest: under the eye of Mr Holt, though, the caretaker had to take punishment and, very determined, he headed with her for the door. But he really needed ten arms, not two.

"Can I open the doors for 'im?" Miranda asked.

"Please do!" Mr Holt was wiping his forehead with his hankie. "Then straight back here." He was breaking all the rules. Miranda wasn't allowed to go anywhere in the school on her own.

She opened the door, managed a stroke of the struggling cat while she was at it, and off they went — while Mr Holt sank back onto his cat-furred chair with a look on his face which said he wished it were home time.

6

Mr Toombs tried to lose Miranda on the way. He tried different grips for carrying the cat which might leave a hand free for the doors, but he just couldn't manage. He tried asking various children who were out of their classrooms to do her job instead, but none of them were going to cross Miranda Finch: not at the risk of a push in the face or a kick on the leg.

"Wassup with you?" Miranda asked him. "I can do it, can't I?"

He said nothing to that, but Miranda reckoned she knew what his game was. He didn't want her to know where he was going with the cat. He was scared that if she knew, she might come back later and do something horrible to that cat and her kittens. She had a name for hurting and she was proud of it. But as if she would! To an animal!

"Which way?" she kept asking after every door. "Which way?"

And he kept bluffing. He kept stopping, looking for other helpers, waiting for her to go away. "Thanks, love. Ta, that'll do. I can manage from here." But she wouldn't have it. She stayed with him, kept putting a hand up to the cat to show how she wouldn't hurt it. And by the time they'd gone down three flights of turret stairs, through three sets of swinging doors, she knew where they were going anyway. Not through the halls to a spare room. Not across the playground to the caretaker's house. They were going down to Mr Toombs's little kingdom, the boiler room, the place down the stairs past the notice painted on the bricks:

NO PUPILS BEYOND THIS POINT.

She was glad about that. The cat would like it. It was good down there – she knew, because she was one of the pupils who *had* been beyond that point. Twice. Once, when she'd been down there on her own for a snoop around, something to do instead of going to the lavatory in lesson time. And once when she'd been shut in there for five minutes after she'd gone wild in the playground

– and it was the handiest place they could keep her while they called for Mr Holt.

Yes, the cat would like it. It was cosy, a little den, with a shiny floor and a bare desk and the easy chair which matched the one in Mr Holt's room, only in better condition. And it was lovely and warm. The gas boilers hissed and hummed, and made you feel quite sleepy: the best cut-off bits of classroom carpets were nice and soft and there was a radio playing *The Jimmy Young Programme*. She wouldn't have minded living there. And it was definitely a good place for a cat to have its kittens.

Mr Toombs kicked a cardboard box out of a corner and dribbled it over to one of the boilers. "Take that out of there," he said, "and bung in some of them rags."

Miranda removed the few bars of soap which sat in the bottom and put them on the caretaker's chair: she found the rags the man was nodding at in someone's P.E. bag hanging behind the door; and she made a comfortable nest for Charlie and her kittens.

Gently, Mr Toombs let the cat down into it. And with his back to the door and waving Miranda away, he watched the box and waited to see what his cat would do.

She must have been tired because she didn't do much. She jumped out once, walked all round it, and jumped back in; then she padded round ten or twelve times and laid herself down. This time she didn't lick and preen herself; she didn't close her eyes and sleep. She laid there, eyes open, staring at the inside of the box: and waited.

7

"Well, I ain't got all day," said Mr Toombs.
Which was a laugh, because he usually had. He
turned to Miranda. "An' you've got to get back
upstairs. Straight back."

Miranda didn't budge. "I'll 'ang about. See
she's all right."

"Oh no, you won't! She don't need you! She
needs a bit of peace and quiet. Besides, it ain't
right."

Miranda stared at him: she'd seen things born
and she'd seen things die: more than him,
probably. But she knew he wouldn't let her stay.
Nicola Ward could have stayed. Or Wendy Kent.
But the name Miranda Finch definitely wouldn't
allow it.

"Bring her some milk, playtime, can I?"

"She'll have milk. You leave her be." And Mr
Toombs counted her out of the boiler room like
the last customer out of the Co-op.

It took her twenty minutes to get back to the office. Mrs Spencer-Craft nodded her in to Mr Holt's room, the door ajar. Miranda was such a frequent visitor in here that the secretary didn't even bother asking if she could go in when Mr Holt was alone. It was like a passport Miranda had. All the same, she sat back in her chair and covered the typewriter with her arms as the girl went past.

Inside the head's room things were back to normal. Mr Toombs had been back and helped Mr Holt tidy up, and the headteacher himself seemed to have education on his mind again.

"Where have you been, Miranda? Mr Toombs has been up and gone."

But she didn't answer: and he didn't really expect it. If there were an injured child lying somewhere he'd have heard about it by now.

In any case, Miranda was very determined not to tell him what she'd been doing, until he found out for himself — if ever he did.

8

It was a long morning, and the morning ran on into the afternoon. Apart from having her dinner at a table with Mrs Winterburn and then walking round the playground in the tight hand of a dinner lady, Miranda did nothing except be a bit of furniture in Mr Holt's room. They had got the maths done somehow − all by Mr Holt, Miranda hadn't really got hold of it − and she'd read a page of a book to him. But from then on he'd been too busy at his desk, and she'd been left to colour in a picture. Being 'sat on': being kept out of everyone's hair.

By three o'clock she had got so bored that she had even forgotten that morning: looking up at Mr Holt, picturing him with his backside stuck out didn't make her laugh any more. Her mind had gone off in a Peter Pan and Wendy world where she had a house of her own like the boiler room, lots of children to look after who she could

bash when they were naughty: and a husband who
bought her Smarties, and chips. It was that
quietest of Dockside School times, after play in
the afternoon, when Mrs Spencer-Craft had
already gone home and before the parents got
laughing in the playground. In the distance the
lorries rumbled to the Blackwall Tunnel and an
aeroplane came over low to the City Airport, all
drone; which was suddenly disturbed by the door
to Mr Holt's office swinging noisily open –
squeaking, because all the doors in the building
squeaked since Mr Toombs had run out of oil.

Miranda looked up. Mr Holt looked up. Only
out of curiosity, nothing frantic. Was it a nervous
infant with a message? Or a quiet mother come to
apply for free meals?

It was Charlie, Mr Toombs's cat. Not pregnant any more, not fat and bulgy, but thin and frail, walking on rubbery legs and looking weak. And in her mouth, held by the scruff of its neck, was a damp black kitten, dangling helpless as the mother cat swung it round the door.

All at once Mr Holt looked like someone in Madame Tussaud's: not a visitor, but on the waxen side of things. Miranda stared, didn't need to put her felt tips down because she hadn't been holding any. Both of them watched as the cat came in and soft-footed her way along the fireplace kerb and across to the lower cupboard door.

It was shut. So slowly, no panic, Charlie turned her head – the kitten still in her teeth – and looked up at Mr Holt.

Mr Holt looked back at her.

"Open it, then!" Miranda hissed. Mr Holt obeyed, and backed away.

Charlie laid her kitten in the space in the cupboard she'd chosen before, on the bare boards now that the nest had been cleared. And with her head held high, and quite fast for her fragile state, she ran back out of the room.

"Aaaah . . .!" Mr Holt turned to Miranda, put his head on one side, spoke in a whisper, looked near to a tear. "She's brought me a present. She's given me one of her kittens."

"No, she ain't. You wait!"

They didn't have to wait very long. It was only a matter of minutes before Charlie was back again, with another kitten in her teeth, dangling like before. Once more she went to the cupboard, put the second kitten next to the first, and trotted out of the room again.

"Well, I'll be blessed. One for you, is that?"

Miranda shook her head. "No, mate. Got some old paper? Any old bits of rag?"

"Why, why . . .?" But even while he was asking questions, Mr Holt was helping Miranda shred government papers he could manage without.

"This is her nest, see? Where she chose. Not down the boiler room. This is where she's gonna feed 'em."

And, one by one, the kittens came. In through the door and into the cupboard; which, by this time was warm and cosy with the nest made inside it by Miranda and Mr Holt.

9

"How did you know? Have you seen this before?"
Mr Holt seemed quite impressed with what
Miranda had told him.

"Yeah. One done it once in my dad's car.
Picked a Vauxhall, wouldn't have nowhere else."

"Forever smitten! And what happened?"

"Drowned the lot, didn't he? My dad!"

"Well ..." Mr Holt tried to draw a veil over
that. "But you remembered, eh?"

"That's why I opened the doors, fixed 'em back
with things. It's what I was doing. Bet myself
she'd have a go at this."

Mr Holt raised his eyebrows. "And you won!
You were right. Then we'll have to give Charlie
what she wants, won't we? And you can help her
with them, eh? Bring them their milk? Do the
dirts tray?"

"Yeah, if you like."

"While you're good, mind, only while you're
good."

Miranda stared back: didn't nod, but didn't shake her head.

"And there's a lesson, isn't there?" Mr Holt went on laughing. "Have you noticed? Charlie can count! See that? She's counted her kittens and brought them up here one by one." They watched the cat. Five kittens were squirming in their nest, but Charlie was going back for another. "There's a challenge for you! The cat can count but what about Miranda?" He'd put on his teacher's face.

"No, she can't. She can't count."

And Miranda was right: because the next time Charlie came back her mouth was empty.

"She only kept going back till there weren't no more down there. S'not counting."

Mr Holt shrugged his shoulders. He wasn't

sure. "Anyhow, are you going to get her some milk? The kittens have got her milk, but she'll need some . . ."

Miranda got up. Charlie was in her nest giving herself a clean-up after the birth, while two or three of the tiny meowing creatures were trying to cling to her little teats.

"Got a saucer?" Miranda asked.

"*Please*! No, not on me. Go down to the kitchen and ask the cook. Tell her I said."

Miranda flopped her weight, put her hands on her hips. "I'm not allowed down the kitchen. She'll do her nut. I've got to be with someone else."

The headteacher looked her in the eye. "I'll buzz her. Go on, you can go on your own. I'll tell her ... I'm trusting you."

Miranda straightened up. "You ain't, are you?"

"Yes, I am. Can I?"

"Dunno." Miranda bent down again to look at the cat and her kittens, Charlie protecting the little ones like a proper parent should. "She don't trust no-one. I don't." And when the girl looked up, her eyes said *Why should you?*

But he let her go all the same, and she came running back with the saucer and a carton of milk. And nothing happened to anyone she met on the way, there or back. That time: which was a first. And it was a start. Of course, there was no way Mr Holt could tell whether or not Miranda would change her old habits. Charlie hadn't been prepared to alter her ways, had she? Not for him. All he could do was look on the bright side – which he had to, being the head of Dockside School.

MORE WALKER PAPERBACKS
For You to Enjoy